LIGHT AND DARK DOORWAYS

CONTENTS

Light and dark Doorways — 1
Chapter 1 The Storm — 7
Chapter 2 The Job — 11
chapter 3 The Doorway — 15
Chapter 4 The Adoption — 20
Chapter 5 The Story — 23
Chapter 6 Work — 27
Chapter 7 Before the Invasion — 31
Chapter 8 The Sphere — 34
Chapter 9 The Light — 37

Wilbert F. Webb

Light and Dark Doorways is a work of fiction. Any similarities to Individuals, living or dead are coincidental.

All rights are reserved and No part of this work may be reproduced In or by any media without the expressed permission of the author.

First printing August 2019

Copyright 2019

Wilbert F. Webb

CHAPTER 1 THE STORM

On a bright and sunny morning in the middle of May Adam, who had just recently celebrated his 13th birthday, was out for a walk. Adam liked to walk the woods and be in tune with nature. On one of his many excursions, and he had many, a thunderstorm approached and Adam was in the middle of a large field without protection. The storm came quickly and Adam knowing the dangers with lightning strikes, and he could see many as it was a severe, very severe lightning storm, one, which he had not experienced before. As he looked all around, he could see no shelter and he was open to danger and without any protection. Adam was calm by nature so he started to walk and took the path that he knew would take him home to safety. After walking a minute or two, lightning struck the ground in front of him and arced in a circle around him. Adam could feel warmth and a tingling in his body and knew he was feeling something he had not felt before.

He fell to the ground and became hot with cold chills at the same time, lost consciousness, his head was hurting and his vision was blurred. Not knowing how long he had been there when he awoke the sky was clear without a cloud and the storm had passed. Well, Adam did not feel badly at all. In fact, he felt rather energized. Adam continued walking, as he was still several miles from his house, and arrived there being happy that he survived the storm.

His mother, Anna, greeted him when he got home. "Adam, where were you during that terrible storm?"

Adam replied, "I was in the midst of it. I was in a field with nowhere to go and lightning struck close by and I could feel its warmth and I was not sure whether I was going to live but I did and I feel good so the lightning did not do any damage".

Adam's mother hugged him, as she was very happy, knowing what damage lightning could do and how it could have severely damaged or even killed him. She was very protective of Adam, especially since her daughter Evelyn left home looking for work two years ago and had not been heard from since. She told him to go get some dry clothes and clean up, and she would fix him a nice meal, as it was approaching suppertime.

As they were eating the storm returned and the lightning struck again just outside the house. The lightning again circled but not just Adam but it encircled the whole house, the lights went out and both Adam and his mother were in fear. The storm passed and did no apparent damage and Adam told his mother that is what I went through mom by myself out in the middle of that field so we both were lucky that we were not hurt.

The next morning Adam went to school and he walked as he normally did because the school was only a few blocks from his home. His day was typical until he we started his math class of which was not one of his favorite classes. The teacher had a quiz that day on what the class had been studying for the past week and put questions in pre-algebra on the blackboard and asked the class to write the answers down on a piece of paper and when they had the answer they could leave and leave the answers on the desk. Without even thinking, Adam wrote two answers down, put the paper on the desk, got up, and left the room which Adam's teacher thought very unusual, as Adam was not a good math student. She knew Adam always had problems learning but he could learn. Knowing Adam was a serious-minded young man she just did not know what to think when he wrote the answers down, got up, and left the room. She waited until all the students finished and left the classroom then picked the answers from Adam's desk and sure enough, Adam had written down the answers correctly. This intrigued the teacher and she just did not know what to think but she would ask Adam next time she saw him.

When Adam came in the next day—and he always came early—the teacher took him aside and said, "Adam, how did you do those two math questions so quickly? You were the first one done."

Adam said yes he was even surprised himself but when he looked at the questions on the blackboard, they just seemed to be easy and as he read them, he understood exactly how to do the problem.

The teacher said, "That is great Adam and let us hope it continues". There was no test that day or the rest of the week.

At the end of the day, when Adam returned home he talked to his mother and told her something good has happened. "You know I am not good at math, but last week when the teacher put two math questions on the blackboard, I knew the answers at once. I was the first one done and during the week when I read my math assignments, they were easy too.

In fact so easy I did not need to read each word as I just scanned over the words and they all became clear as what to do. I am sure the teacher will be surprised on the next test we take as I think I know pre-algebra almost by heart".

Adam knew there was something different about the way he now knew things. In addition, the teacher and his fellow students were becoming aware of his abilities, especially a fellow student, Devon, who did not like Adam and he told the teacher he thought Adam was cheating.

Adam was not used to all this attention and the thought of his friends thinking he cheated was hard on him. Therefore, he instinctively started to act the way he learned before and his teacher and fellow students soon treated him again like good old

Adam as Adam was a nice kid and everybody liked him. Everybody except Devon who seemed to be jealous of Adam.

As time went on Adam excelled in all his classes but never let on and even purposely missed questions on tests so his test results would be average with his class. As Adam was in the seventh grade, he would need to hide his abilities for five more years and even though he thought at the time this would be difficult, those years did pass quickly. Adam still tested as an average student even though his learning abilities at school and at home very high on all subjects. Adam and his mother often talked on the subject of his mental abilities, where and why he had them.

After graduation, Adam revisited the field where the lightning had hit close to him and it was a clear June afternoon. Almost to the exact spot in the middle of that open field, storm clouds were upon him, very dark and full of lightning flashing vertical and horizontal across the sky when a lightning strike hit the ground in front of him and arced in a circle and he was in its center, just like what had happened five years prior. This time when Adam awoke from the physical stress of the lightning hitting close to him, he realized his senses were elevated to the point where he visualized his mother in the kitchen, baking bread. He also was aware if he were only to think of a place his mind he could go there with the timeline being now. As he sat cross-legged in that field he knew he could also levitate, read minds, and do things that no human before him has been able to do. He knew there was a reason for all these gifts and abilities but was not sure what they were and where the future was going to take him. He would just return home and tell no one as he thought strongly about this.

CHAPTER 2 THE JOB

Even though Adam was cautious, word got around that he was special, smart, and getting a job was never going to be a problem. A local scientist, Bob Carter, who was working on several technical projects, needed an assistant who was fluent in trigonometry, have a creative mind and be willing to explore beyond the known and accepted scientific methods, and Adam applied for the job. The two, understandably communicated very well with each other and Bob hired Adam on the spot as they talked about, explanations that incorporates laws, hypotheses, and facts and theories of gravity and evolution, etc. Adam did not tell Bob about his abilities as Adam knew this was not to be.

Adam did well working with Bob as Bob challenged Adam with complicated tasks and this kept Adams mind active. Even so, Adam knew something more was to be for him as his mind swirled with many thoughts. Now and then, his mind drifted about his sister Evelyn and why she did not keep in touch and he knew his mother was saddened.

While working on a project Bob had given Adam, he came across to a folder marked portals realms and transfers. Adam opened the folder and read it in its entirety. Adam was fascinated as it was descriptive with theory where as another realm was thought to exist. In addition, movement between the two realms was possible.One of the pages in the folder had complicated formulas to accomplish that. The folder had a date on the cover July 1887, which was 63 years ago. If the date was relevant to the contents of the folder then someone other than Bob was working on this theory. That evening I saw Bob and asked him about the folder I had found and read. Bob said he had forgotten about that and it was a theory his father was working on. Bob said his father was obsessed with movement between two realms and worked many hours on that project. I asked Bob if he would mind me looking over the notes more thoroughly so I could better understand his father's thoughts on that subject. Bob said, rather nonchalantly, "sure help yourself".

Adam at first was just inquisitive but the more he read Bob's father's notes and worked some of the formulas he realized what Bob's father was working on was possible and he started to expand on the theories that were in the folder. One of the theories in the folder, written in the present, which I thought unusual as thinking and formulating in the future would be more acceptable thinking. There were stories, which described the rays of the sun to contrast with shadows creating portals and it reminded me of something Jules Vern would have written.

Adam left work and was driving along with the sun beams being very strong and even to the point that made him squint looking out the windshield. He passed under the shadow of a large building and during that time, he felt strangely different as if he was somewhere else. When he emerged out of the shadow that strange feeling left him like walking in and out of a cold shower, the difference was that noticeable. Was being in the shadow of the building causing this feeling? Was it a period of time that would have happened anywhere Adam was? Adam had time to check this out because the sun was strong and slowly setting. Adam turned right at the next intersection and then right again and then right again so it would position him on the street where

Light and Dark Doorways

the shadow was. As he approached the shadow, he now was aware what possibly could happen. When he entered the shadow, again that same feeling came over him and now he knew, it was because of the shadow, but the why was still unknown. When Adam left the shadow that strange feeling left him as before. This time rather than driving around the block as traffic was light; he backed up into the shadow and again was overwhelmed. This time he stopped the car and pondered what he would do next.

The car was in a position to accept the light from the sun as it slowly set. As the sun touched the hood of the car, the color went from white to blue, which was the color of Adam's car. In addition, because he was in the shadow while driving for such a short time he had not noticed the color change before. With each movement of the suns path, the car, consumed by the sunlight until it was total blue in color again. It was like being in two different places at the same time slowly leaving one and entering another. The building shadow was then gone and everything was back as it was before. Adam continued going home and pondered what just happened. The next day Adam drove again to the building with the shadow only this time he parked his car before entering, got out and walked to the edge of where the shadow was.

He watched as pedestrians entered the shadowed area, left again, and did not notice anything unusual. He then entered the shadow and again that strange feeling came over him. This time as he was within the shadow he watched the people come, go, and even had conversations with some of them.

What he did notice was his clothing was different before he entered the shadow. It was obvious to Adam; he was the only object that changed when he entered that space. He looked around the shadowed area and there was only one doorway there. Adam was not sure what would happen when the suns movement would un-shadow where he was. He quickly entered the doorway because it had its own shadow but did not open the door. Not knowing what would happen if he stayed there within the shadow of the doorway when it became un-shadowed from the suns rays, he decided to walk out before that happened.

Always being observant, nothing was unusual, shadowed or un-shadowed so again reinforced his thoughts that he and only he is affected. That night as Adam was almost asleep he remembered the writings of Bob's father about sun and shadows and his theories about moving between two realms.

The next day Adam returned but this time he decided to stay when the area became un-shadowed to test what would happen and be thinking more about Bob's father's theories. Adam stood there within the shadowed area and watched the people come and go and watched the shadow slowly ever so slowly

un-shadow where he was as the suns ray approached. As the last glimmer of grey disappeared and my heart racing as his adrenaline was in high gear not knowing what was going to happen. Nothing did happen except, his clothing, which had changed color when he entered the area changed back as he looked, before.

Adam then concluded that once entering the shadowed area he could stay there and explore where that doorway would lead him that he previously just walked up to, turned around, and left. He also observed while being within the shadowed area and observed the people's movements and no one ever entered or came out of that doorway. No one other than Adam changed by the presence of the shadow and no one was using the doorway, and then the doorway must be for him to enter. Adam considered the doorway was not visible to others so he asked people within the shadowed area to describe what they saw where the doorway was and they said, "a red brick wall", so that did confirm the doorway was only visible to him.

CHAPTER 3 THE DOORWAY

The next day as before Adam entered the shadow and proceeded directly to the doorway, which he entered. It looked like any other area with a vestibule with a long hallway attached. Walking down the hallway, with entrances to rooms with people working doing clerical functions or other like activities I decided to enter one of those rooms and start up a conversation. I was creative and asked a young woman if she knew where Mr. Davenport was working and she said she did not know a person by that name.

I chose the name Davenport because it was an unusual surname and if I used a Smith or Jones name there was the possibility that someone by those names would be working there and I did not want that to talk to someone, as I was just observing. I noticed the clock on the wall and it was the same time as my watch. Everything looked normal except for the clothing I was wearing and that still puzzled me. I then asked if today was Tuesday the 30th and the woman acknowledged with a yes sir. Down the hallway, an exit door entered a street area with a sidewalk, I left the building, and making sure, I knew exactly where I was for the trip back. I saw what looked like a hotel with a restaurant attached and as I was hungry and tired, I had a good meal and decided to stay the night.

When it came time to pay the bill, not thinking, I used my credit card, it was rejected, and when I attempted to pay with cash, they refused the money because it looked like play money to them. I apologized and assured the manager I was not trying to defraud them and as a gesture of good faith, I removed an expensive ruby ring from my finger to hold until I returned to pay them. He accepted, I left, retraced my steps and went home to ponder this mystery. I then noticed my ring was on my finger again and I just gave it to the restaurant manager for collateral on my unpaid meal. I had no idea how that just happened. I decided to return with some items of value and pawn them for cash so I could function within this place, as it was different from where I lived.

I was in another dimension as a place where money had changed, my credit card denied; it could be the only explanation. I gathered a few things of value and returned but as I attempted to enter the doorway, the objects I was going to exchange for cash fell to the street and would not pass with me through the doorway. It was now clear if I was going to function within the new realm I needed to earn money in that realm. I returned to the restaurant, let them know I was unable to get cash to pay them, and asked if I would be able to wash dishes to pay my obligation. The manager said that would be fine but the ring I gave them as collateral was missing. I then realized the ring, being from my world would only be visible if I was wearing it. As I waited for the manager to tell me what to do, a man approached and struck up a conversation.

He said, "I could not help but notice what was going on and I would be happy to pay for your meal. You look to me like you are not from here" and I replied, "that is correct". "How about a nice cup of coffee", the man said and I said, "okay" and we went to his table. I let him do most of the talking, as I knew nothing about this place and could not have a knowledgeable conversation with him.

Looks like I will need to go to the local library and learn about this place so I can look like I belong here. The man told me his name was David Willson, Second National Bank manager and gave me his phone number.

He then asked me about my clothes because the style was different and said, "did you just come through the doorway portal"? I was dumbfounded because I did not expect him to question me about that. I paused, and then with an eagerness to talk to someone who knew what I was going through, I said,"yes".

David got a big smile on his face and then changed his expression back to being more serious. He said he came through the portal 10 years ago and is unable to leave. It seems once you enter this realm you are here forever.

Here is some money to help you settle in your new home. Here you need to be very careful as a dictator governs us and the police are aware of newcomers to the area.

Just then, Adam said to "David, several men are approaching and they look like police". David turned and scanned the restaurant area and said, "Where, I do not see them" and Adam replied, "Trust me they will be here shortly". Just then, the police entered the restaurant and moved quickly to the table where David and Adam were sitting.

When they reached them a police officer with a hand held piece of equipment started to scan Adam and at that time I instinctively said to him, "stop scanning"... He paused and then turned the scanner off, pushed a button after raising the scanner to his mouth and said, "it was a false reading and everything here is okay". He apologized to me for the inconvenience and he and the other police left the area. After they left David asked me, "what was that"?, "What did you do"?

I told David about my experience, being in close proximity to a lightning strike and after that; I noticed that I had gained the ability to learn at a fast pace, faster than normal, and other unexplainable abilities. David said, "You would do well here". I said to

David, "You tell me that once you are here in this realm you are unable to return where you came from, but that is not the case for me as I have been back several times". There are problems though as only what was on my person when I entered will pass back through the portal. David said, "then you could bring a weapon or anything with you and that would pass freely"? I said, "I think so as long as I am touching the object. I do not know how a weapon would work coming from one realm to another".

David and Adam left the restaurant and proceeded to the bank where David worked. As David was a vice president, he was able to hire Adam and this would give him funds to function in his new environment. David also let Adam know he wanted to leave this realm and return home but he did not know how. David asked me to look up his business partner, Bob Carter when he returned home, as Bob, was also a friend who could help getting David home again. I said to David, "you are not going to believe this but I work for Bob". That gave David a chuckle and strengthened his resolve finding a way to pass back through the portal. I mentioned to David about finding the folder on realm travel using a portal written by Bob's father back in 1887. David said he also read the folder and that using one of the formulas he was able to enter this realm but the formula would not let him return. Something Adam did with the formulas that David did not do was allowing movement between both realms. David still remembered the theory number for the one-way movement and told it to Adam. Adam said he would look at it and see if he could figure where David made his mistake.

The next day when I went through the doorway to return home and the money David gave me dropped to the vestibule floor. I forgot the money was in my pocket and would not pass so I went back, picked up the money and will hid it in a book that was on a desk in the vestibule and started my trip home again.

I talked to my boss, Bob Carter and explained to him the unbelievable story and meeting his business partner David Wilson in another the realm. So that Bob would believe Adam, David told me things to tell Bob that only he would know.

Bob and I talked for hours about what happened to me and meeting his business partner. Bob told me David did not show up for work one day, ten years ago and no one knew where he was or what happened to him.

I told Bob everything that happened with the lightning and the abilities I now had. I told him about being able to command the police officer in the other realm to stop scanning and he did so at once. I also told Bob I was able to pass freely between the realms with what I was touching.

Bob told me he and David studied different dimensions theories and travel from his father's files and knowing that David had succeeded was amazing. I told Bob that David and I talked about how he passed through the doorway portal using one of his dad's theories.

That evening I went home, told my mother, Anna I would be out of town for a while and asker her not to worry, but knowing my mother as I do she would anyway.

CHAPTER 4 THE ADOPTION

Now that Evelyn was gone and Adam leaving, Anna thought it was the time to tell Adam about the adoption. She explained to Adam me and your father lived off the grid with their closest neighbor being 10 miles away. We had no children, were self-sufficient, as you would need to be living off the grid. One morning a knock came at the door, which was unusual as we rarely received visitors. When I opened the door, I saw two children, one in a basket of very young age, which was you Adam, and a small girl, your sister, with a note pinned to her coat. I quickly and instinctively picked up the basket and whisked the young girl into the house as being unattended where we lived was dangerous because of the many wild animals. Evelyn looked to be around five years of age and you Adam no more than six months old.

You were asleep and I placed you on the sofa, I removed the coat from the Evelyn and asked her where her mother was and she just stared at me not making a sound. It was around suppertime and darkness came early where we lived. I asked Evelyn again a question about her mother and she still did not utter a word as her eyes roamed around the room knowing she was in a different place. I said to her, "what is your name"? There was no response

Light and Dark Doorways

from her so I said, "I will call you Evelyn for now". I always liked the name Evelyn as I had a favorite aunt with that name.

I sat Evelyn at the table and placed a bowl of soup, with bread in front of her as that was the meal, we were having, and she started to eat finishing the whole bowl. I asked her if she would like more and she smiled and said yes which made me very happy. I can see Evelyn was tired and sleepy. I took her to the guestroom, a room that we rarely used, laid her on the bed and soon she was fast asleep. I returned to the living room, and you were still sleeping, I dare to wake you as surely you would start crying. Let us call you Adam for now, not knowing your birth name and as you and your sister were new to me, Adam, and Evelyn seemed appropriate names.

Everyone settled in and I needed to read the note that was pinned to Evelyn's coat. The note read; my name is Mary and I cannot go on. A falling tree killed my husband and I buried him. I do not have any family or anyone to turn to and without my husband; I cannot take care of my two children. A poisonous snake also bit me and even though my resistance is great, I fear I am going to die. Please do not look upon me as being a bad mother. I love my children very much and want the best for them and this I know I cannot give them. I am going to the city, never to return because the memories are haunting to me. I drew a map to our house for you to get anything there and to help my children adjust.

Anna and her husband John could not have children and they were willing and eager to start a family so they accepted the responsibility and would raise Adam and Evelyn as their own.

The next day John and Evelyn went to your home to see what they would take back with them to help your and Evelyn adjust to your new living arrangements. Evelyn looked around and finally spoke and said, "Where is my mommy"? This saddened John very much as he knew Evelyn would never see her again.

He told Evelyn her mother was away, that he and his wife Anna would now be taking care of you and your brother Adam and she was not to worry. Evelyn seems content that someone was going to care for them. John, with the help of Evelyn gathered clothing for Adam at her and any furniture that was worth saving and to comfort Evelyn.

Evelyn then did something, almost supernatural. She stared at the table, cupped her hands as if she were to pick something up and an object silver in color appeared. It was metallic, smooth on the surface with out any handles or openings. She then picked up the object and placed it with the belongings we were taking.

I asked Evelyn what just happened and she told me her mother said if anything ever happened to her I was to retrieve the sphere, as it will protect us. I said okay but how did you make it appear out of thin air? Evelyn said her mother had taught her how to do things like that. John was amazed at the girl's talent but kept a low-key attitude, as he would ask her more about it later.

We returned home and Anna and I talked. I told her what Evelyn made appear and how she did it and about Evelyn's mother telling her never to leave it behind if anything ever happened to her. We agreed this was not normal and not from our time and Evelyn and Adam were not from Earth. We decided to adopt Adam and Evelyn, and return to the city where the children could be better cared for and educated. We know a young couple who was anxious to live off the grid and when we told them our plans to return to city life and they offered to buy our house. Within two months we were moving with our new family back to civilization and it was exciting for us as we always did want children and Evelyn was excited too. It is hard to believe how fast time has gone by and now with Evelyn gone and you going away, we are saddened.

CHAPTER 5 THE STORY

One night as Anna was tucking Evelyn into bed and she said, "Do you know any bedtime stories". Anna told her about Goldilocks and the three Bears, The Ugly Duckling, Cinderella, Snow White and many others. Evelyn said her mother told her a special story but it was nothing like the stories that Anna told. Anna asked Evelyn, if she remembered the story and would you tell me. Evelyn smiled and said sure. Anna started her story and called it Home. The story first was like a poem and mother said I needed to think about the story not to just listen to it. I liked my mother to tell me the story although thinking what the story was about was hard for me but mother said it would be clear when she was older and not to forget it.

We move in freedom, we move in mind, Nothing to slow us, our thoughts are pure. We travel from here going to there, with nothing to bind, our thoughts are pure. Some time ago, as the vastness was, never ending, never ending where I was, and we searched for freedom, which surely is. My travel friends and the ones I love moved freely searching ever searching. We moved in and with the light and avoided, the darkness as it weighed heavy on our search for freedom. We were coming, my travel friends and I; we were going, my friends and I searching ever searching as we raced through the unknown. We searched for goodness as we thought it would be, we searched for freedom my friends and me, we ran from the darkness it was not to be. Like a rope or glue binding us there, breaking free was hard and told impossible. Having faith my friends and me, we moved forward and crossed the vastness never ending never ending. Chased by darkness to renew its hold, chased by darkness cold ever so cold, chased by darkness through the vastness never ending, light, light, light is our friend. Soon we found our freedom, soon we found our light but darkness was always nearby. We took the form, as it is here; we took the form and were pleased. Here you replenish although with an end but your spirit goes forward never ending, never ending. As my travel friends and I were born of thought, here to be born is different and we are happy and content. We found our freedom as guided by the light and we are happy and content.

Anna told Evelyn she enjoyed her story. I think your mother was telling you of her beginnings, as I believe she was not from here and neither was your father. Your parents were good people and I wish John and I knew them in person. As you get older Evelyn, you need to keep your talents and the story a secret as the people here on earth would not understand and telling them about this could put you and Adam in danger. Anna said good night to Evelyn and said sweet dreams my little darling. She then went to Adams room, tucked him in and told him she loved him very much and to always be with your sister.

That night Anna told John the story Evelyn told her and John agreed with Anna... Adam and Evelyn were not from Earth but from another place within the universe. He also agreed the children should never tell anyone. Adam told Anna he was thankful for her and now had an understanding after listening to his mother's story.

Why he was here and how he got here is no longer a question. Adam then returned through the portal and retrieved the money he had hidden in the book and proceeded to the Second National Bank where he wanted to meet up with David. As he approached the bank, he saw unusual activity and police were everywhere. He inquired with a passerby and asked what was going on. The government had taken over the bank and the assistant bank manager arrested. David was Adam's only contract and he needed to get David free. They were holding David at the local police station so Adam decided he must act quickly before they transferred him to a larger facility. David walked into the local police station and told the officer behind the desk, he was to release David Willson in his custody immediately. The officer promptly went to the cell where David was, unlocked the cell door and asked David to follow him. David was surprised to see Adam but remembered what he had done in the restaurant to the other police officer and surmised Adam did the same thing here to get him released. They quickly left the police station with David taking the lead and Adam followed him. Cameras were everywhere and after going a block or two, David went into a building with Adam close behind. The building had many rooms and was most likely an apartment David went to the second floor, and opened a door and we entered.

David and I changed clothes to disguise ourselves. The back of the apartment had a fire escape, which took us to the first floor, and we proceeded on foot. We soon reached another building that had a garage attached, that contained a car. We drove for several hours, and entered a road that was narrow and winding through the heavily forested area and we entered what looked like a compound as it had several buildings and armed guards. David parked the car and several people approached him and talked in a whisper. David said to one of the men who he called Philip, "it is okay Philip this is my friend Adam who is one of us".

We went inside one of the buildings and took a secret elevator down many stories. When we reached the bottom and exited the elevator, we were in a room with a lot of electronic equipment and people listening and monitoring and to me it looked like I had entered, what I perceived a CIA area would look like.

David and I brought Philip up to date on what was happening with David's arrest and escaping with my help. Philip told David and Adam that the police were very active and arresting anyone who looks suspicious to them and did not have class I credentials. I asked Philip what class I credentials were and he said," if the police had given you a background check and took your DNA then you were considered class I". I asked Philip how the police determined who was a class I when checking and he told me, "it was required of all citizens to keep with them a copy of their certification". "Do you have a copy of a class I certification that I could look at", I asked Philip and he said he did. He went to a table, opened a drawer, retrieved it, gave it to me, and said, "I know where you are going with this thinking Adam but having a copy of one is not enough, as it cannot be duplicated. When you attempt to copy it, the copy becomes bright red and unusable".

Adam looked at the original and saw a small implant on the paper that not only prevented copies it also had a failsafe that if someone altered this prevention a GPS locator would activate. I suggest finding a copy machine at a location not used by any of us, make a copy and at once pour acid on the original to destroy any fingerprints and the GPS locator. I would then leave that area quickly. Now you will have a good duplicated class I credential form.

Philip assigned this task to one of his trusted members and shortly he returned with the new class one credential form. I placed in our copying machine, and made 10 copies without incident. David and I now had class one certification to use if ever stopped.

CHAPTER 6 WORK

David and I found work within the local government and I used my mind-altering talent to advance us within the hierarchy. We chose this work to keep us informed on government activities. I asked Philip if he was born in this realm. He told me this is the only place he has ever known and then the invasion came and everything changed for us. Our government as we knew it was quickly overthrown and our president and leaders put in prison and now dictator rules us.

David and I talked about the two realms, agreed they were separate, and kept that way and we must help Philip and his friends restore his government. Before we could do anything with this realm, I needed to find a solution on returning David Willson. I asked Philip where the invaders came from.

Were they from another government from within this realm and were there other governments that could invade also? Philip could not answer those questions, as this is the only place he has ever known. I also asked Philip if there were maps drawn so they could travel. Philip said the best place to find that information would be at our library and I remembered, I was going to visit and get informed on this realms culture and yes, that would be the place to look.

The next day I went to the library and asked the librarian where I could find any maps. She said maps…."That is an unusual re-

Wilbert F. Webb

quest as nobody seems to have interest with maps, but they are located in our archives in the rear". She walked me to the room and retrieved a large binder, which was full of maps for the area and then left. Shortly thereafter, a police officer approached me and said could I see your credentials? I gave him my class one credentials and after looking them over, he said thank you and left the room. How he knew I was there is a mystery to me, possibly are there cameras in the room, or did the librarian alert them? As I looked at the maps, I noticed they were all the same with different acreage and all rectangular in size with the city square being in the center. The earliest map was 1 acre in size and dated July 1887. The maps updated in no particular point in time with the latest dated July 1950, and had increased in size to 100 acres. It is possible this realm is not physical and grows or decreases in size based on how many people currently live here.

After reviewing the maps I knew the invaders came from within or outside this realm as no other lands were visible. I returned and talked to Philip about my thoughts on this matter. I asked Philip if he could remember anything unusual during or just before the invasion and as Philip was thinking, he did say a terrible electric storm was present with much lightning, horizontal and vertical striking the ground all around us.

I remembered the same type of storm as Philip was describing happens to my mother and me and to me alone in the open field and shortly after I realized I was different. This was something to think about and if the storm was the cause of the invasion and the invaders were already here then the storm changed some of the locals who then took over imprisoning members of the local government. Adam remembered the story his mother told to Evelyn's and it is beginning Poem.

We move in freedom, we move in mind, Nothing to slow us, our thoughts are pure. We travel from here going to there, with nothing to bind, our thoughts are pure. Some time ago, as the vastness was,

Light and Dark Doorways

never ending, never ending where I was, and we searched for freedom, which surely is. My travel friends and the ones I love moved freely searching ever searching. We moved in and with the light and avoided, the darkness as it weighed heavy on our search for freedom. We were coming, my travel friends and I; we were going, my friends and I searching ever searching as we raced through the unknown. We searched for goodness as we thought it would be, we searched for freedom my friends and me, we ran from the darkness it was not to be. Like a rope or glue binding us there, breaking free was hard and told impossible. Having faith my friends and me, we moved forward and crossed the vastness never ending never ending. Chased by darkness to renew its hold, chased by darkness cold ever so cold, chased by darkness through the vastness never ending, light, light, light is our friend. Soon we found our freedom, soon we found our light but darkness was always nearby. We took the form, as it is here; we took the form and were pleased. Here you replenish although with an end but your spirit goes forward never ending, never ending. As my travel friends and I were born of thought, here to be born is different and we are happy and content. We found our freedom as guided by the light and we are happy and content.

Adam's mother and father both thought he and Evelyn were not from Earth and I agree. The story our mother told to Evelyn, I believe has the answers and possibly the solution to get back home.

As my travel friends and I were born of thought" ...

Was my mother actually saying she was born of thought and if this is true could the invaders be part of the travelers who came to earth as she mentioned the darkness and chased by them? She said she traveled with her friends so chased by darkness means there were others and they were not friends.

I believe some people of this realm are from the darkness or the darkness is the invaders who followed Adam's mother as they traveled going from here to there. She also asked Evelyn not to forget the story and she would understand what its meaning was

Wilbert F. Webb

when she was older.

CHAPTER 7 BEFORE THE INVASION

I asked Philip if he and his friends were happy before the invasion and he said, "Yes, everything was peaceful and we were happy". I told Philip I was not sure why David and I were here with you Philip but there must be a purpose. I truly believe our goal should be to expel the invaders and restore the leaders to office that are imprisoned. Philip said that would be great if we could get back to the way we were before the invaders came. I asked Philip if he knew how many and where the invaders were. He said he did not although they gathered once a month at an unknown location for some type of rejuvenation that I understand is required to keep them healthy. With my ability to ask and they obey I can find that information so we know they all will be in one place monthly.

Later that day I approached a police officer and asked him when and where the next rejuvenation date was and he told me it is always the first Monday of the month and we will meet in the local Coliseum at 1 AM. It is doubtful we would be able to do anything in 20 days, which would be the first Monday of next month, but what is firm is the first Monday. We need to find out just what happens to during rejuvenation, as this seems to be their Weakness. If we can stop this from happening, will they cease to function or go back to another form that we can control? I will be there during the next rejuvenation and see what actually goes on.

Adam went to the Coliseum on a Wednesday afternoon, when they were least busy and did a walk-through. He did not see anything unusual or any equipment to use for the invaders rejuvenation. There was a place in the building that had little activity and Adam could view most of the Coliseum from that location. On the Monday in question, Adam arrived at 11 PM so those attending would not notice him. He watched and waited and around 12 AM people started to enter the building. They all took a seat with little fanfare or chat they waited for the appointed hour. When 1 o'clock came something from their pocket, placed it on their right temple, and went into a trance like state. Because they were not alert, I went as close as I could, and with caution looked for any activity that would look like rejuvenation and I saw none.

I left the building before they became alert and pondered what he had witnessed. The next day Adam met with David and Philip and let them know what happened at the Coliseum. Philip received a report from his monitoring unit, they advised him of a strong signal was transmitted at one AM that Monday, and it came from the Coliseum. Maybe the information about the rejuvenation was not correct and what was actually happening was a transmission. Upon further examination, it was determined the transmissions gave precise location information.

This was troublesome and opened the possibility of more invaders coming. That night the police arrested Adam and wanted to know why he was at the Coliseum? Adam told them he was restless that night and seeing the lights within the building, he entered because he was curious. They took him to the prison because he is a political risk and they placed him with others with the same charges. Adam could have willed himself free whenever he wanted to but he wanted to see what they were going to do with him. At the prison, he quickly found the president and members of the local government that were imprisoned. He talked to them with caution, as he was not sure if they were who they said they were. I was thinking they could be a plant by the invaders to get information from me. One of the local government imprisoned leaders asked me if I would be willing to talk to a woman, also imprisoned, who had much the same views as he did. I said I would and a time and place was arranged for me and the woman to meet. As I entered the meeting place, I was shocked seeing my sister Evelyn and when she saw me, she felt the same, but subdued, as she did not want, anyone to know they were knew each other. Evelyn told Adam she entered the portal doorway when she was looking for work not knowing she was entering another realm. She took a job with the local government about the time of the invasion, and arrested.

The police abused her new friends but she was able to stop the abuse with her powers and decided she could not leave them or they may be injured or killed. That is why she stayed could not get word to her parents that she was safe. Adam understood and said mother and dad were well and they missed you. I brought Evelyn up to date on where we were with the invaders and let her know the end plan to get rid of the Invaders, restore the local government to power and return home.

CHAPTER 8 THE SPHERE

Evelyn told Adam she has instructed Anna to talk to the Sphere, and say to it, "**born of thought** " and to repeat those words until the Sphere glows, if I was ever missing for a longer period of time than six months and that date was approaching. You need to go back and let mother know I am ok and not to talk to the Sphere unless you here me in your mind asking you to do so. Adam questioned his sister and asked why she could not telepathically talk to the Sphere? Evelyn said the instructions needed to be from a local source. I also asked Evelyn what the Sphere would do after receiving the instructions, "**born of thought**". She said the Sphere would find me wherever I am and protect me.

Adam summoned a guard and instructed him to release him and remove the records to show he was never here. I left the prison, talked to David and Philip letting them know I was going back through the portal and why and that I found my sister in prison. She was an employee with the local government and taken captive by the invaders. I returned, talked to Anna about the instruction to the Sphere and explained Evelyn would give her new instruction telepathically. Anna wanted to know how Evelyn was and I assured her all was well and we would both be home

Light and Dark Doorways

in the near future. Before returning I talked to Bob, letting him know what was going on in the other realm and the possibility an invasion of earth and both realms is possible. As I entered the doorway, the police were waiting for me... I told them not to arrest me but my command was ignored.

My powers were not working, and that now is very serious as without them escaping would be very difficult. They took me directly to the prison and placed me in a holding cell with an armed guard. Shortly after, I arrived two men entered the room and asked questions.

> What is your name?
>
> Why are you here?
>
> Do you know a David Willson?
>
> Do you know a man named Philip?

How did they know about David and Philip, as these were friends only known to those within our group? They did not ask me about the security complex and I was certain I did not share this information with anyone other than David and Philip in conversation.

This to me indicates a mole in our presence. I was thinking how they knew the exact time I would pass through the doorway portal. In addition, if that was a factor that would narrow the choices of people who knew that information. It was not long before Evelyn heard rumors of my arrest and put a plan in place to free me. Evelyn retained her powers and that night she made her way to my cell, told the guard to release me, which he did and they both left the prison and met up with David and Philip.

An attempt to determine the mole within our ranks narrowed from a few people to one person. If we were correct with our choice then our innermost circle is in jeopardy. We must verify our choice as not knowing for sure we could not move forward with our escape plan and the plan to restore the local government. We decided Evelyn would make contact and share fake information, but important information that the mole would pass on, if indeed our choice was correct.

We absolutely had to know, as this person is important with our decision making process. We let it known that an important meeting was to be held at a specific date and time and with its location. Our plan was to watch for any one monitoring or approaching the meeting site and then we would know the mole passed on the information. To keep confidence we would tell the mole the meetings cancelled just before it was to start therefore not giving the mole time to pass that information on before we could verify anyone monitoring or approaching the meeting site. The information about the meeting, now given to the mole and we were correct with our suspicions. Police activity is higher now than at any other time according to David and Philip so something important is in the making.

David, Evelyn and I wanted to leave this place but we knew we had to remove the invaders and put this realm back to where it was before the invaders came. The police were looking for us and we took refuge at the security complex and made our plans. More invaders were on their way, we had a mole at our highest ranks and Adam's powers were gone.

CHAPTER 9 THE LIGHT

The next meeting for the invaders was approaching and we knew they would be transmitting again and we could not let this happen. The local Coliseum was the only meeting place that was large enough to accommodate the invaders as a group and we suspect by being together their transmission power magnified as a group when they put that object from their pocket on their temple.

The Coliseum stood alone and away from other buildings, so burning it to the ground was our best option. We decided not to do that but thought of ways to capture the invaders. There were many, too many for our group unless we captured them one at a time. Sedating them and removing the object that they put on their temple was an option. It was also an option to let the invaders in the coliseum and wait for them to go into their trance during transmission and then gas them and before they awakened, take the temple object from them if possible.

While all this planning was going on at the security complex the alarm sounded, which indicated we were under attack and we needed to escape quickly. We had a plan in place if this ever happened. We headed for the exit to safety when the doors opened and the police with no way to escape surrounded us. Shackled and placed in a security van, driven back to the prison, and once there securely locked in a room with no windows. Everything we did failed, as the invaders were always a step ahead of us.

When alone Evelyn attempted to release us from our shackles but to no avail as she also had lost the power to do this. Evelyn tested each of her gifts to see if anything was available, first she attempted to levitate and that failed. Then with telepathy tried and she was able to contact Adam so not all was lost. She felt impressed to look beyond the walls of the room. When she did this, she saw Bob Carter sitting in a chair, not alert and a figure standing over him that was void of facial features.

Evelyn's mother told her about this image and she described it as being the darkness. Then the darkness walked toward Bob and entered his being like a grey mist and Bob awakened.

This was new information. I thought now the invaders were the darkness, taking over local citizen's bodies, and changed their will.

Bob Carter was our mole and now I know why. I remembered the story my mother told me as a young girl and said when I got older she said the story would be understood. I remembered...

Chased by darkness to renew its hold, chased by darkness cold ever so cold, chased by darkness through the vastness never ending, light, light, light is our friend.

It was now clear what we needed to do but how to do it. We needed to remove the darkness from the people and replace with the light. They took us to the coliseum that night with all the invaders present and displayed us as to take pride being the victors. They spoke with confidence how the dark side was triumphant and together nothing would be able to stop them. Then the leader, who was speaking, announced to the group, punishment... "Dark punishment must be given to those before you to caution the light to stay away and dark punishment means death". Evelyn knew it was time to send for the sphere and she used her thought transference to her mother. Evelyn repeatedly told her mother… Go to the sphere; go to the sphere, and say, born of thought, born of thought, born of thought.

The invader leader then turned quickly and raised his hands saying to Evelyn, "Stop what you are doing" but Evelyn continued using her thought transference, sending her thoughts to her mother. The Invader leader then said, "Stop or I will cut your head from you body" but Evelyn continued because she knew the Sphere was their only rescue. The invader then turned to his group, removed a device from his pocket, raised the device above his head and turned back toward Evelyn, David, Adam and Bob. The device was a weapon not seen before and was very powerful. A swirl of mist churned around its cold steel frame and Evelyn could see the evil within. The leader moved forward toward them, pointing the device and chanting, "Darkness all powerful protects us from the light". Evelyn summoned all her spirit to stop what was about to happen but she could feel her body being drained and nothing she did could stop it. Then the mist encircled her and expanded to include Adam David and Bob. Then you could see their images change and blend within the mist itself as if to become one with the darkness.

Another image then appeared within the darkness that engulfed Evelyn and slowly, ever so slowly, you could see a glow, a glimmer of light, growing within and the darkness and silence overtook the Invaders as before they noticed the glow they were cheering for their anticipated victory.

The light grew, larger and larger and brighter and brighter then the grey mist left, leaving Evelyn, David, Adam and Bob with a shield of light to protect them from the imminent battle with the darkness.

Wilbert F. Webb

The light moved directly in front of the Invaders, its glow stayed constantly bright, ever so bright, and as they looked upon the brightness of the light. Then the Invaders who occupied the local citizen's bodies left them as a mist and was drawn into a black hole that just appeared within the coliseum room. Calm returned with the locals never aware what happened to them with their wills changed.

The Sphere, silver in color, smooth and oval, calmly sat on the meeting table without a blush, glow or evidence of its powers except for Adam and Evelyn who knew.

With the darkness gone, never to return and the local citizens, never knowing what happened to them.

Evelyn and Adam with their combined power closed the portal to this realm and they returned home with David and Bob not ever aware what they witnessed.

Evelyn fell in love with a local chap, married and raised a beautiful family. Adam, a few years later did the same finding a local beautiful girl, raised a beautiful family also, and told them about the Sphere, and the story.

"Home".

Made in the USA
Columbia, SC
31 August 2019